A Guest Is a Guest

by John Himmelman

DUTTON CHILDREN'S BOOKS
NEW YORK

Published in the United States by
Dutton Children's Books,
a division of Penguin Books USA Inc.

Printed in Hong Kong
First Edition   10 9 8 7 6 5 4 3 2 1

Library of Congress Cataloging-in-Publication Data

Himmelman, John.
  A guest is a guest / by John Himmelman.—1st ed.
    p. cm.
  Summary: Chaos prevails when the barnyard animals decide to
live in the house with Farmer Beanbuckets and his family.
  [1. Humorous stories. 2. Domestic animals—Fiction. 3. Farm
life—Fiction.] I. Title.

PZ7.H5686Gu 1991
[E]—dc20   90-43020 CIP AC

for Mom and Dad Shanahan

Farmer Beanbuckets, his wife, and their son,
Billy, lived on a farm.

The Beanbuckets were very kind people, and
they always treated their animals like part of
the family.

Billy was especially fond of a clever little piglet named Oliver. The two of them played together every day.

But every night, Billy and Oliver had to go their separate ways.

One evening, Billy asked if it would be all right to have a friend spend the night.

"If it's okay with his mother," said Mrs. Beanbuckets.

Billy went out to the pigpen to get his friend Oliver. All the other pigs were asleep, so he quietly snuck the piglet away and took him up to his room.

Later that night, Oliver's mother noticed that her baby was gone. She woke the other pigs, and they all called for the missing piglet.

The noise woke Oliver. He went down to the back door to see what all the racket was about. The pigs were very happy to see that Oliver was safe. Together they all snuck up to Billy's room.

In the morning, the Beanbuckets came down to a kitchen full of hungry pigs.

"What should we do?" Mrs. Beanbuckets asked.

"A guest is a guest, and we must show them our best," said Farmer Beanbuckets.

Later that day, the rooster saw a strange sight in the farmhouse. He sent in one of his bravest hens to investigate.

When the hen didn't return, he gathered all the chickens together, and they entered the house. They found her on a big, fluffy pillow. It was the softest nest she had ever sat on, and she wasn't about to leave it!

Soon there was a hen on every pillow.

"What should we do?" Mrs. Beanbuckets asked.

"A guest is a guest, and we must show them our best," said Farmer Beanbuckets.

In the evening, the Beanbuckets sat down to watch their favorite western. The pigs and chickens were making so much noise that Farmer Beanbuckets had to turn the volume way up.

The sound of the TV western brought the horses and cows stampeding into the room. They stopped in front of the TV and stared.

"More guests?" asked Billy.

"Afraid so," said Farmer Beanbuckets.

In the morning, there was a knock at the door. It was the ducks.

"I guess they were wondering where every-one went," said Billy.

Now the house was filled with animals.
They took over the TV.

They ate all the good stuff out of the re-
frigerator.

The morning paper was always a mess,

and worst of all, there was always a line for the bathroom!

Finally, Farmer Beanbuckets cried out, "A guest is a guest, and we must show them our best, but when enough is enough, you have to get tough!"

So the animals threw the Beanbuckets out.

Then Billy had an idea. He called Oliver outside to the pigpen. The two of them began to roll and play in the mud.

When Oliver's mother saw them out there,
she led the pigs out of the house and into the
pen, where they could keep a better eye on
the piglet.

This gave Farmer Beanbuckets an idea. He jumped onto a perch in the chicken coop. "Cockadoodleydoo," he crowed.

The rooster didn't like someone else doing his job, and he led the chickens out to the coop.

Mrs. Beanbuckets caught on to what was happening, and she rolled the TV into the stable. The horses and cows followed right behind her.

The ducks were a little more difficult to get out, but moving the tub and shower to the yard did the trick.

The Beanbuckets ran back into the house
and locked the door behind them.

The house was a mess, and after a full day
of cleaning, they were exhausted.

"A guest is a guest, and now it's time for some rest," said Farmer Beanbuckets, and one by one, the whole Beanbuckets family fell asleep.